The Fireless Dragon

adapted by Daphne Pendergrass

Simon Spotlight
New York London Toronto Sydney New Delhi

SIMON SPOTLIGHT
An imprint of Simon & Schuster Children's Publishing Division
1230 Avenue of the Americas, New York, New York 10020
First Simon Spotlight edition March 2015
© 2015 Hit (MTK) Limited. Mike the Knight™ and logo and Be a Knight, Do It Right™
are trademarks of HIT (MTK) Limited. Nickelodeon and all related titles and logos are
trademarks of Viacom International Inc.

SIMON SPOTLIGHT and colophon are registered trademarks of Simon & Schuster, Inc.
For information about special discounts for bulk purchases, please contact
Simon & Schuster Special Sales at 1-866-506-1949 or business@simonandschuster.com.
Manufactured in the United States of America 0315 NGS
10 9 8 7 6 5 4 3 2
ISBN 978-1-4814-2869-9
ISBN 978-1-4814-2870-5 (eBook)

Mike, Sparkie, and Squirt were on a very special mission: They were on their way to get some of Mrs. Piecrust's delicious dragonberry pies!

"Hello, everyone!" Mrs. Piecrust said as they neared her shop.

Sparkie and Squirt leaned in to smell the yummy dragonberry treats that were cooling on the table.

"Mmm!" Sparkie said. "The most delicious pies in all of Glendragon!" He then took a sniff and sighed, but as he did, his fire breath burned every last pie to a crisp!

Sparkie felt terrible.

"Don't worry. It was an accident. But I've run out of dragonberries, so I can't make any more pies today," Mrs. Piecrust said. That made Sparkie feel even worse.

Squirt suggested they go pick some more dragonberries, but it was getting late, and the dragonberry tree was all the way on the other side of the Tall Tree Woods.

"By the King's crown, that's it!" Mike exclaimed as he leaped onto a pile of crates. "My mission is to bring back a basket of dragonberries before bedtime!"

Mike put on his armor and went down the slide to get Galahad. Soon he and Galahad burst out of the stable doors and trotted over to Sparkie and Squirt. When Mike pulled out his sword, it turned into a torch.

"A torch?" Mike asked. "I'm not sure how that'll help us pick dragonberries . . ." But there was no time to lose—they had to get all the way across the Tall Tree Woods before dark!

They didn't get far before Squirt's tummy started rumbling. "Don't worry," Mike said. "I brought something." Mike pulled out the ingredients for hot chocolate, just the treat they needed on their journey! "Sparkie, I'll need you to heat up the chocolate with your fire."

Sparkie was nervous about using his
fire again. "I don't think I want to be a
fire-breathing dragon anymore," he said. "But I
can still be a chocolate-warming dragon!"

Sparkie tried to heat up the chocolate by rubbing the pot
with his hands, but the pot spun out of control and chocolate
spattered everywhere!

"Don't worry, Sparkie," Mike said. "Squirt can give us all a wash."

"Okay, Mike!" Squirt said. He flew over the group and sprayed water into the air, cleaning off everyone.

Suddenly, Mike started shivering. Squirt's water blast had made everyone clean, but now they were cold!

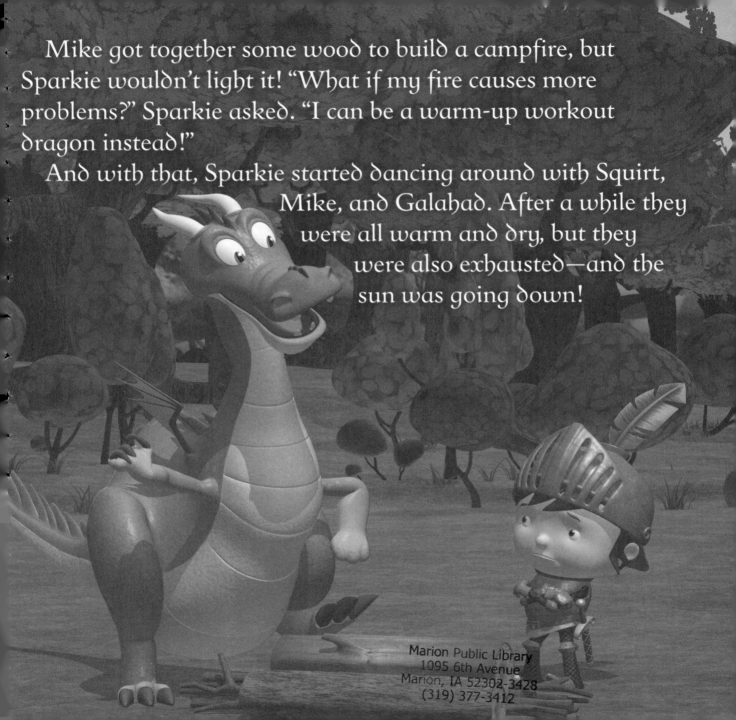

Mike got together some wood to build a campfire, but Sparkie wouldn't light it! "What if my fire causes more problems?" Sparkie asked. "I can be a warm-up workout dragon instead!"

And with that, Sparkie started dancing around with Squirt, Mike, and Galahad. After a while they were all warm and dry, but they were also exhausted—and the sun was going down!

In the Tall Tree Woods, it was getting even darker. Mike, Sparkie, and Squirt couldn't see where they were going, and soon they were completely lost.

"I don't think we'll be able to finish the mission now," Mike said sadly.

"It's my fault!" Sparkie said. "I did burn the pies with my fire, but not breathing fire has only made things worse. . . . It's time for me to do it right!"

Sparkie asked for Mike's torch, and then he used his fire breath to light it. With a little bit of light, they quickly found the right trail.

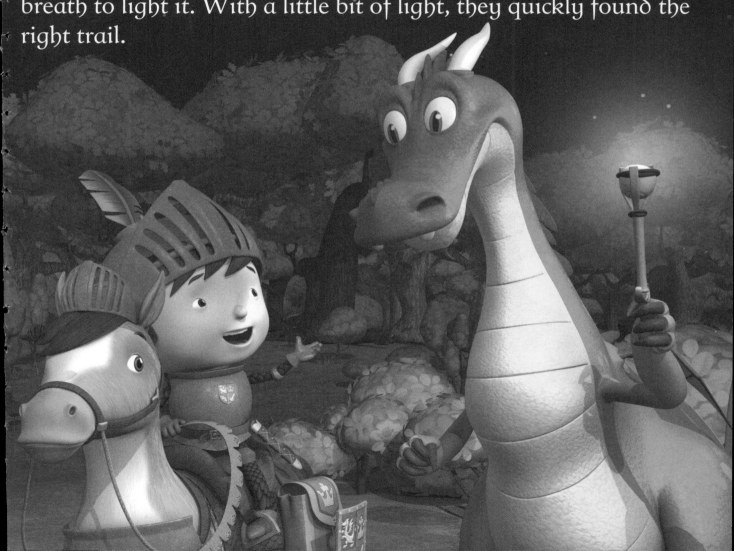

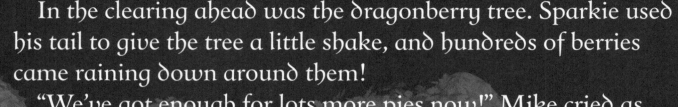

In the clearing ahead was the dragonberry tree. Sparkie used his tail to give the tree a little shake, and hundreds of berries came raining down around them!

"We've got enough for lots more pies now!" Mike cried as he and Squirt filled their baskets. "Lead the way back to the village, Sparkie!"

But when they returned to Mrs. Piecrust's shop, she had bad
news. "I'm sorry, Mike. It was getting late and you weren't
back, so I put the fire in my oven out."

"Don't worry," said Mike. "I know a fire-breathing dragon
who could light the oven superfast!"

"One oven fire, coming up!" Sparkie said.

Mrs. Piecrust quickly baked more
dragonberry pies while Sparkie
heated up a pot of hot chocolate. When everything was ready,
Sparkie laid out the sweets on the table.

"Huzzah!" the friends cheered as they dug into their tasty,
well-deserved treats.

6993